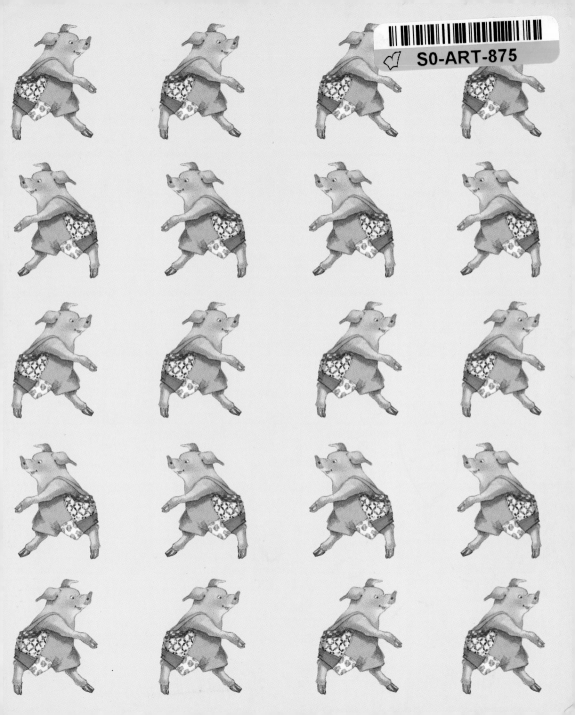

First edition

4 6 8 10 9 7 5 3

ISBN-13: 978-0-7892-0423-3
ISBN-10: 0-7892-0423-1

Library of Congress Cataloging-in-Publication Data
The three little pigs : a classic fairy tale / illustrated by Agnès Mathieu.
p. cm. — (The little pebbles)
Summary: Three little pigs leave home to seek their fortunes and
have to deal with a threatening wolf.
ISBN 0-7892-0423-1
[1. Folklore. 2. Pigs—Folklore.] I. Mathieu, Agnès, ill.
II. Three little pigs. English. III. Series.
PZ8.1.T383 1998
398.24'529734—dc21   97-23044

For bulk and premium sales and for text adoption procedures,
write to Customer Service Manager,
Abbeville Press, 137 Varick Street, New York, NY 10013, or call 1-800-ARTBOOK.

Visit Abbeville Press online at www.abbeville.com.

The
Three Little Pigs

A Classic Fairy Tale
Illustrated by Agnès Mathieu

· Abbeville Kids ·

A Division of Abbeville Publishing Group

New York · London

Once upon a time there were three little pigs who set out into the world to seek their fortunes. The first pig met a man carrying a bale of hay, and he said to the man, "Please sir, sell me your hay so I can build a house with it."

The man sold him the hay, and the first little pig built his house.

The second little pig met a man carrying a bundle of wood, and he said to the man, "Please sir, sell me your wood so I can build a house with it."

The man sold him the wood, and the second little pig built his house.

The third little pig met a man pushing some bricks, and he said to the man, "Please sir, sell me your bricks so I can build a house with them."

The man sold him the bricks, and the third little pig built his house.

Soon after the pigs built their houses, a big wolf knocked on the door of the first little pig's house.

"Little pig, little pig, let me in," the wolf yelled, "open the door and let me in!"

"No! No!" the pig cried, "I'll never, never, never let you in, not by the hair on my piggy little chin!"

"Very well," the wolf replied, "then I'll huff, and I'll puff, and I'll blow your house away!" And so the wolf huffed, and he puffed, and he blew away the little hay house.

And the first little pig had to run away as fast as he could to the second little pig's wood house.

Before long, the wolf arrived at the house of the second little pig and banged on the door.

"Little pig, little pig, let me in," the wolf shouted, "open the door and let me in!"

"No! No!" the pig cried, "I'll never, never, never let you in, not by the hair on my piggy little chin!"

"Very well," the wolf replied, "then I'll huff, and I'll puff, and I'll blow your house down!"

And the wolf huffed, and he puffed, and he blew down the little wood house. The two little pigs had to run away as fast as they could to the third little pig's brick house.

But the wolf followed them to the brick house and pounded at the door.

"Little pig, little pig, let me in," the wolf demanded, "open the door and let me in!"

"No! No!" the pig cried, "I'll never, never, never let you in, not by the hair on my piggy little chin!"

"Very well," the wolf replied, "then I'll huff, and I'll puff, and I'll blow your house to bits!"

And the wolf huffed and he puffed, and he huffed and he puffed some more, and he huffed and he puffed as hard as he could, but the house made of brick stood firm.

Now the wolf was so angry that he decided to crawl down the chimney and gobble up the three little pigs. But the pigs had a pot full of boiling hot water on the fire. When the wolf came down the chimney, they took the lid off, and he fell straight into the pot.

Then the pigs put the lid back on—BANG!—and that was the end of the wolf. And the three little pigs? They lived happily ever after.

Look carefully at these pictures from the story.
They're all mixed up. **Can you put them back
in the right order?**

a

b

c

d

e

f

What do the three little pigs say when the wolf tries to get into their house?

"I'll never, never, never let you in, not by the hair on my piggy little chin!"

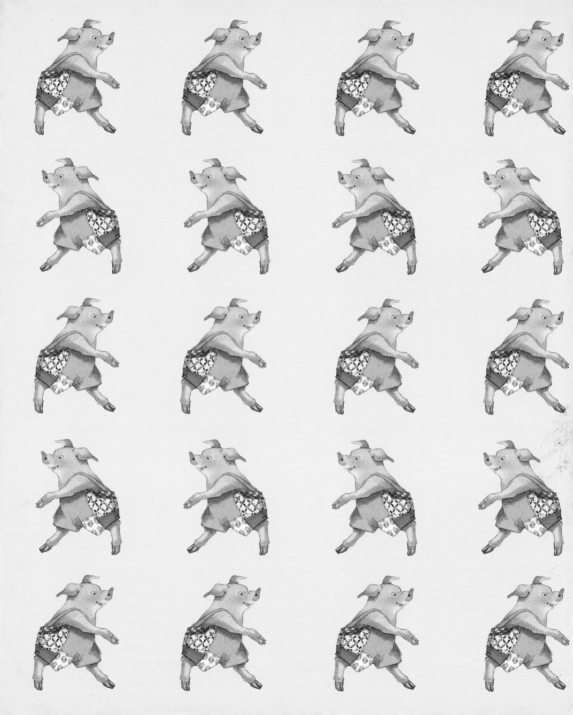